# Angelina Ballerina
## at Ballet School

Based on the stories by Katharine Holabird
Based on the illustrations by Helen Craig

SIMON SPOTLIGHT

An imprint of Simon and Schuster Children's Publishing Division

New York  London  Toronto  Sydney  New Delhi

1230 Avenue of the Americas, New York, New York 10020 • This Simon Spotlight paperback edition June 2021 • Illustrations by Robert McPhillips
© 2021 Helen Craig Ltd. and Katharine Holabird. The Angelina Ballerina name and character and the dancing Angelina logo are trademarks
of HIT Entertainment Limited, Katharine Holabird, and Helen Craig. All rights reserved, including the right of reproduction in whole or in part in any form.
SIMON SPOTLIGHT and colophon are registered trademarks of Simon & Schuster, Inc.
For information about special discounts for bulk purchases, please contact Simon & Schuster Special Sales
at 1-866-506-1949 or business@simonandschuster.com. • Manufactured in the United States of America 0521 LAK
1 2 3 4 5 6 7 8 9 10 • ISBN 978-1-5344-8529-7 • ISBN 978-1-5344-8530-3 (eBook)

D1516424

It was a sunny morning in Chipping Cheddar, and Angelina was very happy. Today was the first day of the school year for Miss Lilly's Ballet School!

Angelina had waited all summer for her favorite ballet classes to start again. She wanted to show everyone the fantastic new dance move she had created over the summer.

Angelina called her new move the Magical Fairy Twirl. It was the best fun ever. She loved waving her wand in the air and spinning around as fast as she could go. She felt just like a fairy casting a magical spell!

Angelina even had sparkly fairy wings she could wear as a costume. Miss Lilly and the other ballerinas were going to be so impressed.

Angelina packed her ballet bag and rushed out the door. She hopped, skipped, and leapt her way over to Miss Lilly's Ballet School.

Everything was just as Angelina had remembered. She went to her cubby and put on her favorite ballet slippers. Then she pulled out her fairy wand. It was going to be a wonderful dancing day!

Miss Lilly called the class to order. "Welcome back, my little mouselings!" she said. "First, let's start our class with stretches and warm-ups."

The ballerinas all took their usual spots at the barre. "Why are you holding a wand?" Alice asked Angelina. "It's a surprise," Angelina said. "You will find out soon!"

After warming up, it was time to dance. "Let's see what everyone practiced this summer," Miss Lilly said.

Angelina raised her hand as high as she could. She couldn't wait to show off her Magical Fairy Twirl.

But first Miss Lilly called on Flora, who performed a dainty arabesque in front of the class. "Bravo!" Miss Lilly said, and everyone clapped and cheered.

Angelina raised her hand high in the air again. This time, Miss Lilly called on her to dance.

"I made up a brand-new dance move over the summer," Angelina announced. "It's called the Magical Fairy Twirl!"

"A new dance move?" Alice said. "Wow!"

Angelina ran over to her cubby to put on her fairy wings. When she reached into her bag, she was horrified to see that the wings were not inside. In all her excitement, she had forgotten to bring them to class!

Angelina made her way to the front of the class, clutching the wand. Without her wings, she wasn't quite feeling like a fairy anymore.

Angelina took a deep breath and began to twirl, waving her wand in the air. But as she twirled faster and faster, she began to lose her balance!

As Angelina wobbled and stumbled, the wand slipped out of her hands and flew into the air. It soared toward William, who scrambled out of the way just in time.

The next moment, Angelina landed on the floor with a thud.

"Thank you, Angelina," said Miss Lilly. "But I'm afraid I can't allow your new move in ballet school until you've done a lot more practice. I don't want anyone to get hurt."

"That was not magical at all," William muttered, looking annoyed.

Angelina felt very upset as she sat down to watch the rest of the ballerinas. The first day of ballet school was supposed to be the best day ever. Instead, it had turned into an absolute disaster!

After class was over, Angelina walked sadly out the door.
She did not hop, skip, or leap back home.

"How was the first day of ballet school?" Angelina's father asked when she got home.

"It was horrible," Angelina cried. She told him everything that had happened: forgetting the wings, almost hurting William by accident, and having her new dance move banned from class.

"I don't want to go to ballet school tomorrow," she sobbed.

"I understand your hurt feelings, Angelina," her father said kindly. "But tomorrow is a new day. You can apologize to William and Miss Lilly. I'm sure they will understand."

Angelina still didn't want to go to ballet school. The next morning, she walked to Miss Lilly's as slowly as she could.

By the time Angelina arrived at Miss Lilly's Ballet School, everyone was already ready for class. She quietly started unpacking her bag, hoping no one would notice her.

Then Miss Lilly walked over. "Is something the matter, Angelina?" she asked. "It's not like you to be late."

"Oh, Miss Lilly, I'm so sorry!" Angelina burst into tears. "Yesterday was all a terrible mistake. The wand wasn't supposed to slip out of my hand. I wanted to impress everyone with my new move, and instead I made a mess of everything and I disappointed you."

"I was not disappointed in you," Miss Lilly said. "In fact, I was impressed by your creativity."

"Really?" Angelina said.

Miss Lilly smiled. "The Magical Fairy Twirl may not have been the safest idea, but I hope you will keep creating new dances. I know that's what you love to do."

Angelina looked up at Miss Lilly and nodded. Then she hurried over to join her classmates.

"I'm sorry about yesterday," Angelina said to William.

"It's okay," William said. "I think it's fun that you made a new dance move. I made one up too. Want to see?"

William raised one arm and started jumping in the air. "This is the bobbing balloon dance!" he said.

Angelina giggled and joined William. Soon, the whole class was bobbing up and down like balloons.

After class, Angelina walked up to Miss Lilly. "I'm going to keep making new dance moves," Angelina said. "But I'll be more careful from now on. When I'm ready, can I show them to the class again?"

Miss Lilly smiled and nodded. "That sounds like a wonderful idea," she said.

"See you tomorrow, Angelina!" William called.

As Angelina waved back, she was already feeling excited for tomorrow. After all, ballet school was her favorite place to be!